W9-BKV-672

DISCARD

NOW THAT IS ONE HAPPY FLOWER!
LET A SMILE BE YOUR UMBRELLA

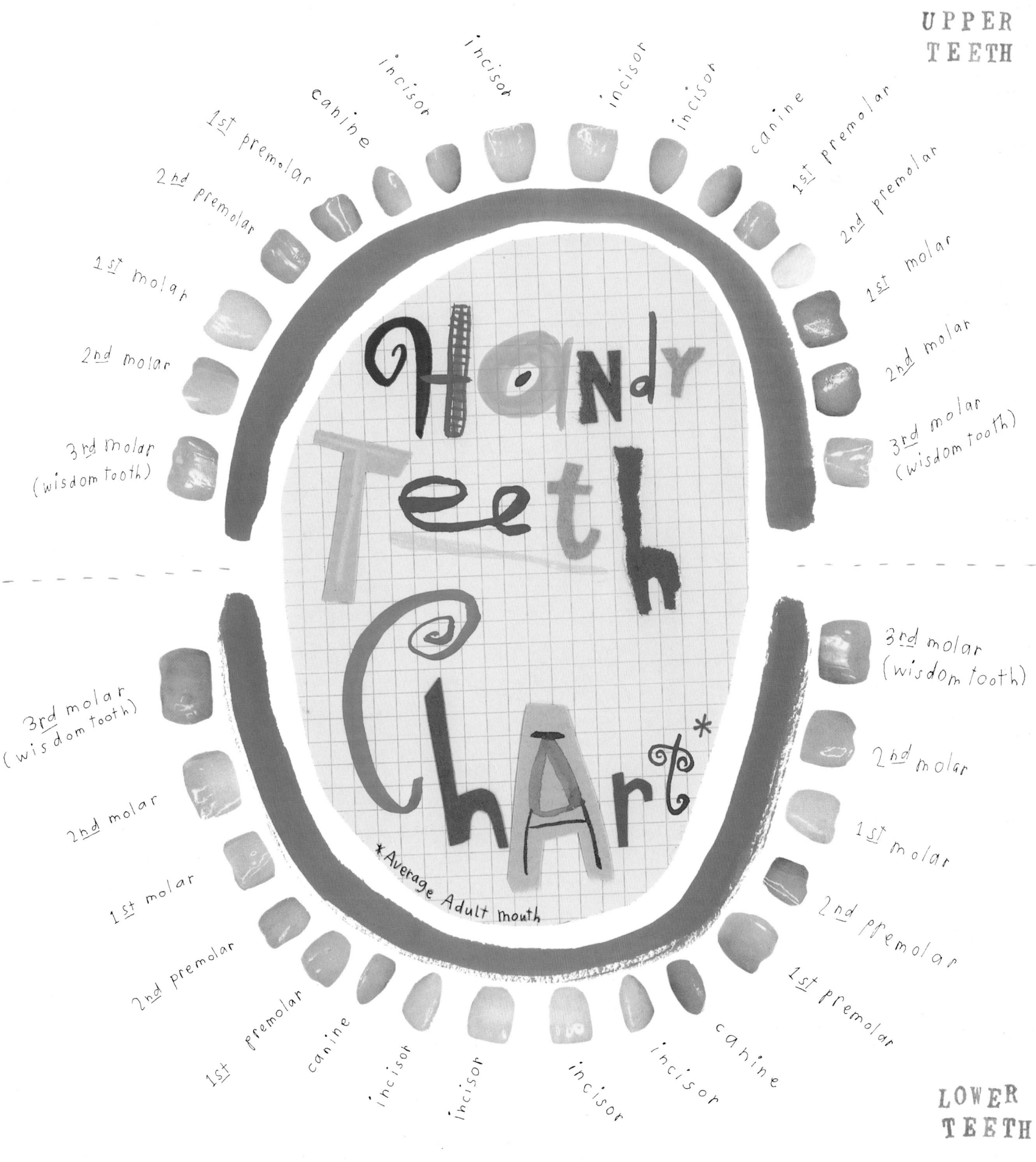
UPPER TEETH
incisor
incisor
incisor
incisor
incisor
canine
canine
1st premolar
1st premolar
2nd premolar
2nd premolar
1st molar
1st molar
2nd molar
2nd molar
3rd molar (wisdom tooth)
3rd molar (wisdom tooth)
Handy Teeth Chart*
*Average Adult mouth
3rd molar (wisdom tooth)
3rd molar (wisdom tooth)
2nd molar
2nd molar
1st molar
1st molar
2nd premolar
2nd premolar
1st premolar
1st premolar
canine
canine
incisor
incisor
incisor
incisor
LOWER TEETH

For my sister, Sherrie

A thank-you song to Christy Ottaviano:
You are the Editing Queen,
always clean, and you're never mean.
(To be sung to an ABBA tune)

The author would like to thank Jill Fernandez at the New York University Medical Center for her help in finding the following resources: *Growing Up Cavity Free: A Parent's Guide to Prevention*, by Stephen J. Moss, D.D.S. (Chicago: Quintessence Publishing Co., 1993), and *Dentistry: An Illustrated History*, by Malvin E. Ring, D.D.S. (New York: Harry N. Abrams, Inc., 1985).

Henry Holt and Company, LLC, *Publishers since 1866*, 175 Fifth Avenue, New York, New York 10010
www.HenryHoltKids.com
Henry Holt® is a registered trademark of Henry Holt and Company, LLC.
Copyright © 2000 by Laurie Keller. All rights reserved.
Distributed in Canada by H. B. Fenn and Company Ltd.

Library of Congress Cataloging-in-Publication Data
Keller, Laurie. Open wide: tooth school inside / Laurie Keller.
Summary: Through a classroom setting in which teeth are the students, this book presents information about the structure and care of teeth and the services provided by dentists.
1. Dentistry—Juvenile literature. [1. Teeth—Care and hygiene. 2. Dental care. 3. Dentistry.] I. Title. RK63.K44 2000 617.6—dc21 99-27965

ISBN 978-0-8050-6182-5 (hardcover) / 20 19 18 17 16 15 14 13 12 11 10
ISBN 978-0-8050-7268-6 (paperback) / 15 14 13 12 11 10
First published in hardcover in 2000 by Henry Holt and Company
First paperback edition, 2003 / Designed by Donna Mark
Printed in March 2010 in China by South China Printing Company Ltd., Dongguan City, Guangdong Province, on acid-free paper. ∞
The artist used acrylic paints, colored pencils, markers, and collage on illustration board to create the illustrations for this book.

Eating popcorn *her teeth* begged for flossing.

R0433420186

Good morning, class.
Good morning, Dr. Flossman!
Sally Incisor
Sam Incisor
Ifa Incisor
Ingrid Incisor
Christy Canine
Carl Canine
Rosie Premolar
Preston Premolar
Pedro Premolar
Boopsy Premolar
Millicent Molar
Roland Molar
Bubba Molar
Melody Molar
Edward Molar III Wisdom Tooth
Wendy Molar Wisdom Tooth
upper teeth
lower teeth
Wallace Molar Wisdom Tooth
Evelyn Molar Wisdom Tooth
Rusty Molar
Marilyn Molar
Martin Molar
Marky "Muscles" Molar
Lola Premolar
Pinky Premolar
Charlie Premolar
Penelope Premolar
Candy Canine
Conan Canine
Omar Incisor
Liza Incisor
ELVIS Incisor
Sherrie Incisor
You're all looking clean and bright today. Let's begin by taking attendance.

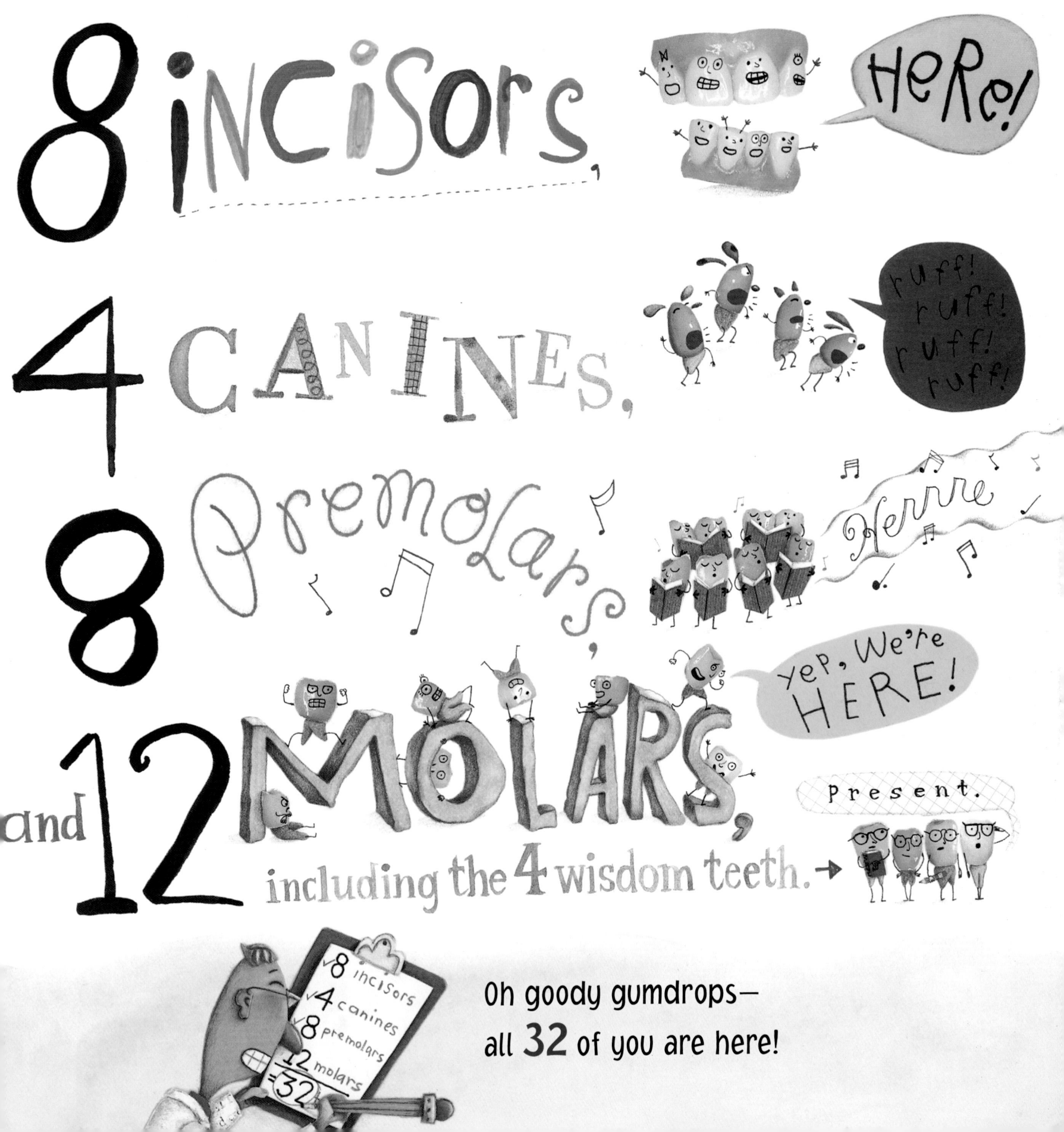

Oh goody gumdrops—
all 32 of you are here!

Before the principal's announcements, would you all please stand and recite our pledge:

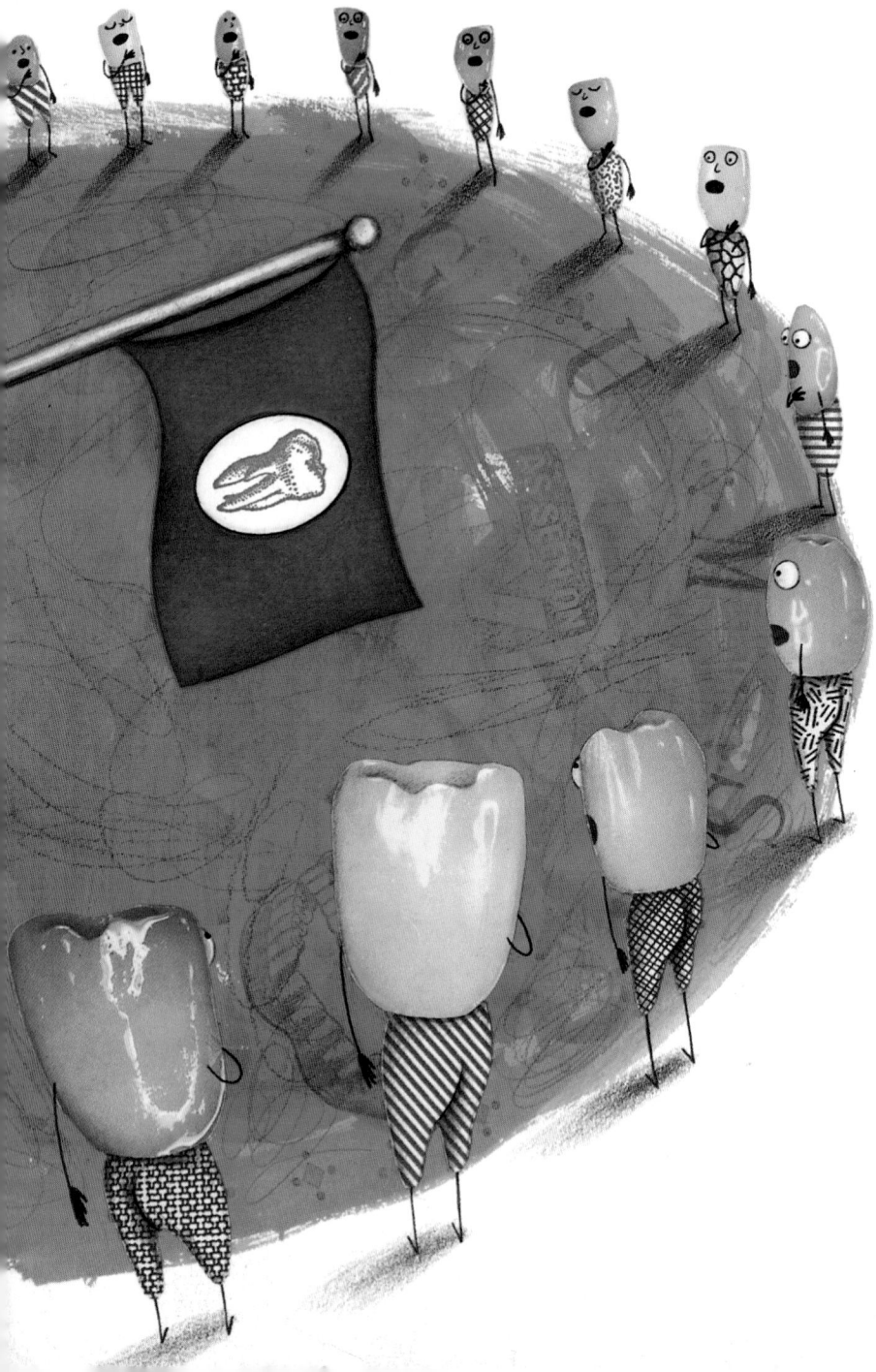

I pledge allegiance to this mouth and to the dentist who takes care of us. And to the gums on which we stand, strong and healthy, with toothbrushes and toothpaste for all.

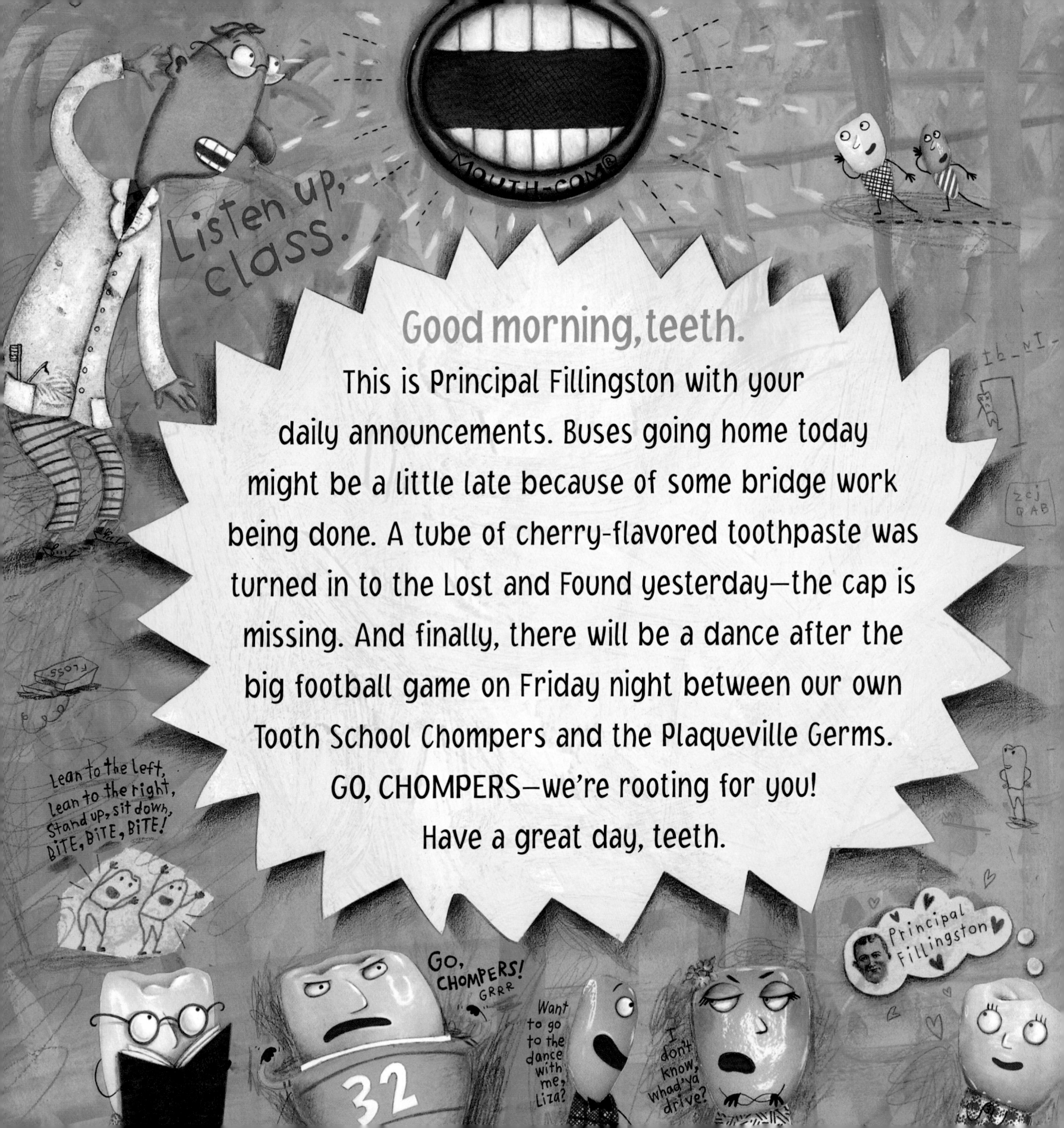
MOUTH.COM®
Listen up, class.
Good morning, teeth.
This is Principal Fillingston with your daily announcements. Buses going home today might be a little late because of some bridge work being done. A tube of cherry-flavored toothpaste was turned in to the Lost and Found yesterday—the cap is missing. And finally, there will be a dance after the big football game on Friday night between our own Tooth School Chompers and the Plaqueville Germs. GO, CHOMPERS—we're rooting for you! Have a great day, teeth.
Lean to the left, lean to the right, stand up, sit down, BITE, BITE, BITE!
FLOSS
Go, CHOMPERS! GRRR
32
Want to go to the dance with me, Liza?
I don't know, what'ya drive?
Principal Fillingston

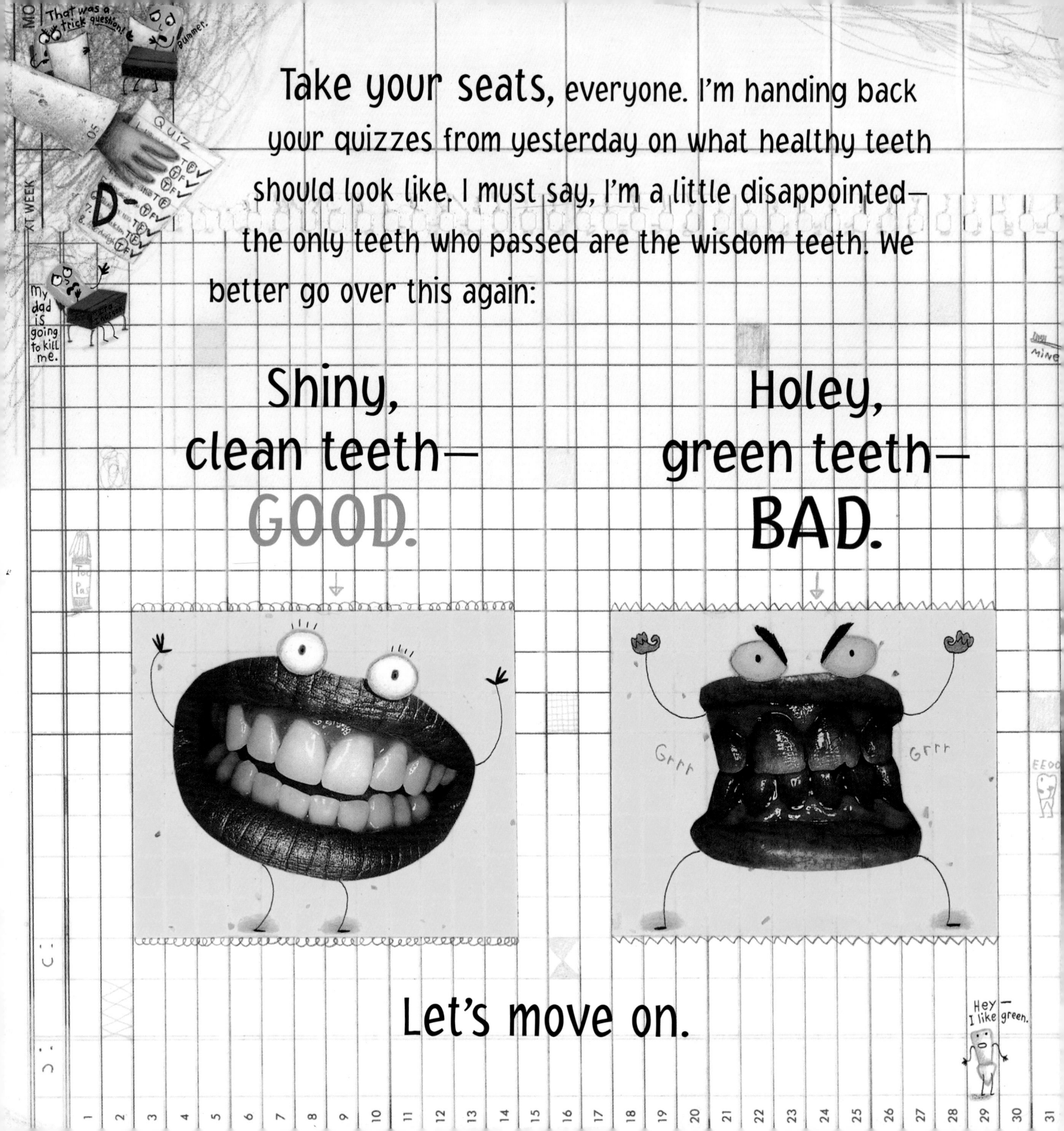
That was a trick question!
Bummer.
QUIZ
D-
My dad is going to kill me.
Take your seats, everyone. I'm handing back your quizzes from yesterday on what healthy teeth should look like. I must say, I'm a little disappointed—the only teeth who passed are the wisdom teeth. We better go over this again:
Shiny, clean teeth—GOOD.
Holey, green teeth—BAD.
Grrr
Grrr
Let's move on.
Hey—I like green.

Here's a look at what you teeth are made of:

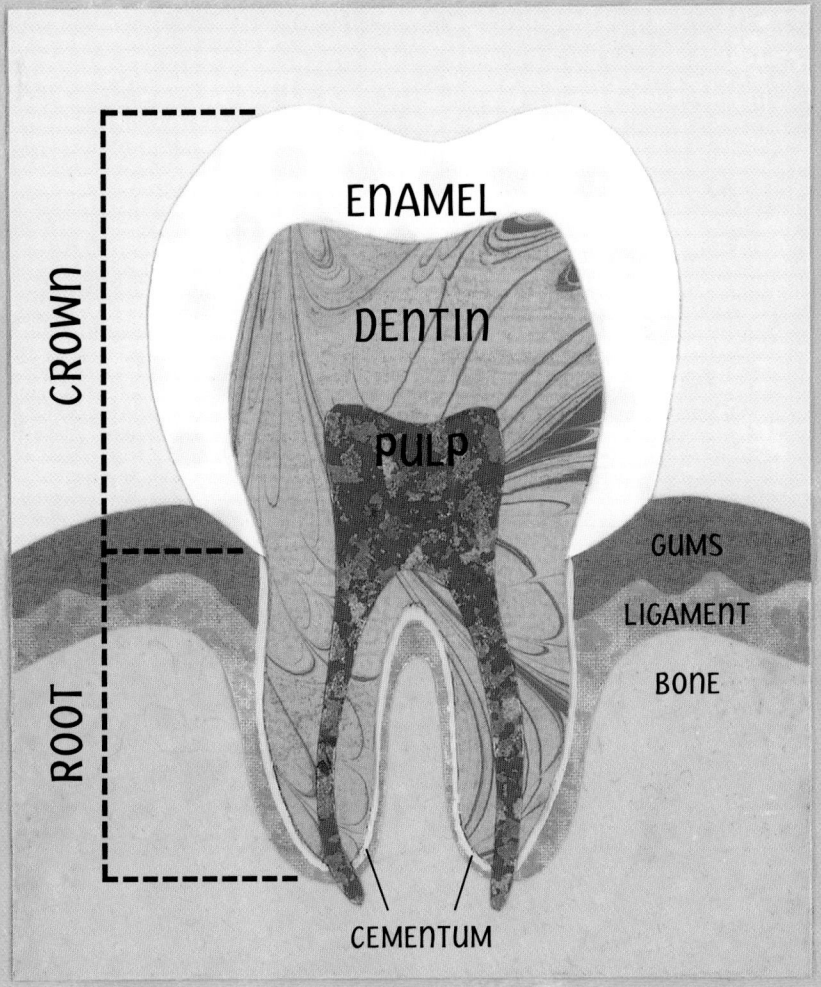

1. When you're in the gums, the part of you that shows is the CROWN.
2. You're covered with a hard layer of ENAMEL to protect you from bacteria and germs.
3. DENTIN makes up the biggest part of you. It's not as hard as enamel.
4. PULP is the softest part. It's what hurts when you get a toothache.
5. The ROOT is what holds you in place. It's protected by a thin layer of tissue called CEMENTUM.

Getting in touch with inner dentin

Bb Cc Dd Ee Ff Gg Hh Ii Jj Kk Ll Mm Nn Oo Pp Qq Rr

Dr. Flossman—
Carl canine called me a
BAD NAME and it hurt my feelings
because even though I have
a hard enamel shell on the outside
to protect me from **bacteria**
and **germs**, it doesn't shield me
from the **bitter sting** of
cruel words...

Okay, class. now we're in for a REAL TREAT.

Sally Incisor is going to read her report on primary teeth.

~~pre~~molars rule!!

CROWN
ENAMEL
DENTIN
PULP
ROOT

Primary Teeth

by Sally Incisor

Primary teeth are also called baby teeth because that's what they are—little, bratty baby teeth. They all wiggled around so much that they fell right out of the mouth until there were none of them left! So us permanent teeth moved in instead. We will be there for a lot longer because we don't wiggle around at all. I don't know why those baby teeth were there in the first place. Babies don't even need teeth. You never see them eating corn on the cob or anything like that. So then after that they go live under a pillow until a toothfairy lady hauls them off somewhere and that is all I know about baby teeth.

THE END.

by Sally Incisor.

Thank you, Sally. Nice job! But actually, babies **DO** need teeth. Baby teeth are **VERY** important for several reasons.

1. They help develop the face and jaw.
2. They help babies chew when they start to eat more solid food.
3. And baby teeth guided you permanent teeth into proper position, and kept the mouth healthy and clean.

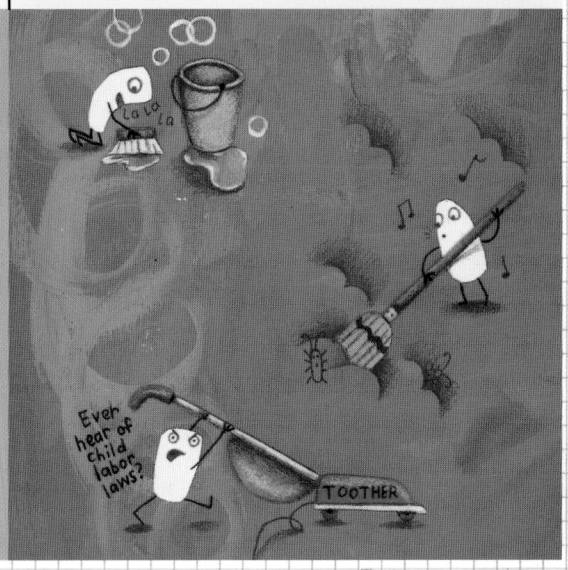

That's real swell, Doc.
But who **is** this fairy of teeth?

Good question, Conan Canine! Let's watch this fun and informative videotape so we can learn more about her.

CANNONBALL!
ARCADE
NO SPITTING OR BITING
FOOD
yum
You got it!
Nice shot! AAhhaaaa
AAAhhhhh
MOLAR COASTER
No hands, yo
MOLAR

MOLAROLA

Hello there,

you cute little permanent teeth!

This is the Tooth Fairy coming to you all the way from Tooth Land. It's my job to bring all the baby teeth here. When a baby tooth falls out, it gets placed under a pillow (which I've never understood—I practically suffocate sometimes trying to get it). After I take the tooth, I replace it with a little surprise—usually money. Then I tuck the tooth under my wing and we're off to Tooth Land!

Well, that's about it for me. Oh—I almost forgot. There are free molar-coaster rides on Tuesday nights, so stop by!

Toodle-do, toothies!

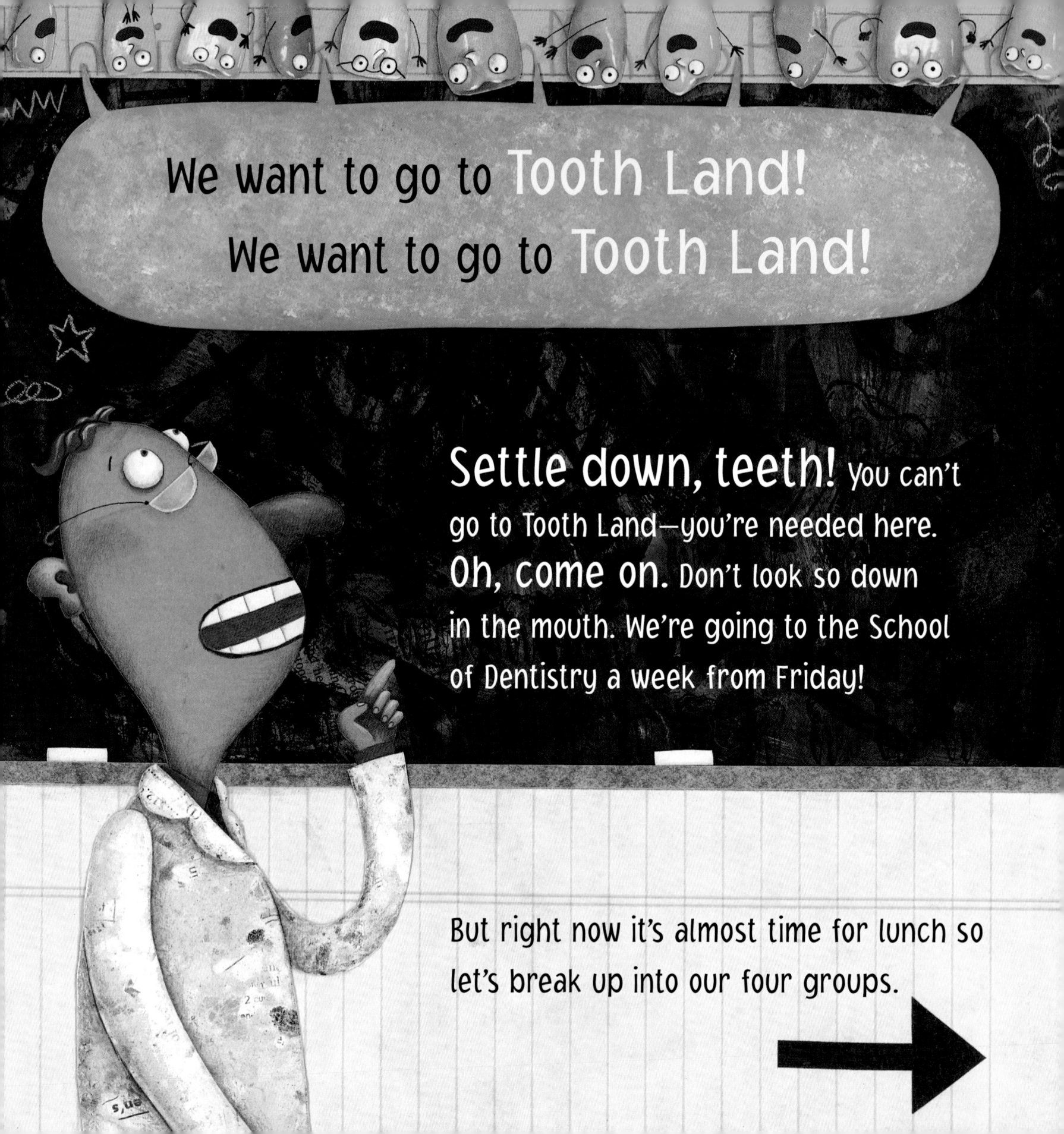

We want to go to Tooth Land!
We want to go to Tooth Land!

Settle down, teeth! You can't go to Tooth Land—you're needed here. **Oh, come on.** Don't look so down in the mouth. We're going to the School of Dentistry a week from Friday!

But right now it's almost time for lunch so let's break up into our four groups.

FOOD CUTTERS

Incisors

FOOD TEARERS

Canines

FOOD CRUSHERS

Premolars

FOOD GRINDERS

Molars

Way to go, class—get in there and **EAT!**

FOOD FIGHT!
Wanna trade?
Oops.
Bet I can run faster than you.
Betcha can't.
Ahhh
Ha Haa
Ha Ha ha
Ahhh Hahhh haa
3 pieces of cake, please. And a pie.
Yuck. I don't like olives.

Ohhh, I'm wedged in again.
Wheeee
FLOSS
Last one there's a rotten tooth!
Hello, boys.
Psssst
Hello, Sweet Tooth.
She thinks she's so sweet.
Yeah.
Where'd he go?

Well, well, well! It looks like you all had a good lunch. But to stay strong and healthy, it's important to brush after meals. So what do you say we take out our toothbrushes and floss, and clean ourselves up?

All right then, class. Since you don't want to brush, why don't we open our books to the chapter on TOOTH DECAY.

Tooth decay is caused by bacteria. Bacteria like to eat sugar. Candy and cookies have one kind of sugar, and foods like fruit, bread, pasta, and milk have other kinds of sugar. Bacteria eat all kinds—especially those that stick to teeth.

(Notice how some foods are not as sticky as they would seem to be.)

NOT VERY STICKY

apples
bananas
hot fudge sundaes

SORT OF STICKY

white bread
caramels
cream-filled sponge cake

PRETTY STICKY

jelly beans
plain doughnuts
raisins

SUPER STICKY

granola bars
oatmeal cookies
potato chips

When lots of bacteria build up on teeth, that's known as PLAQUE. Plaque eats right through enamel. And if plaque keeps eating, it means only one thing—

A CAVITY!

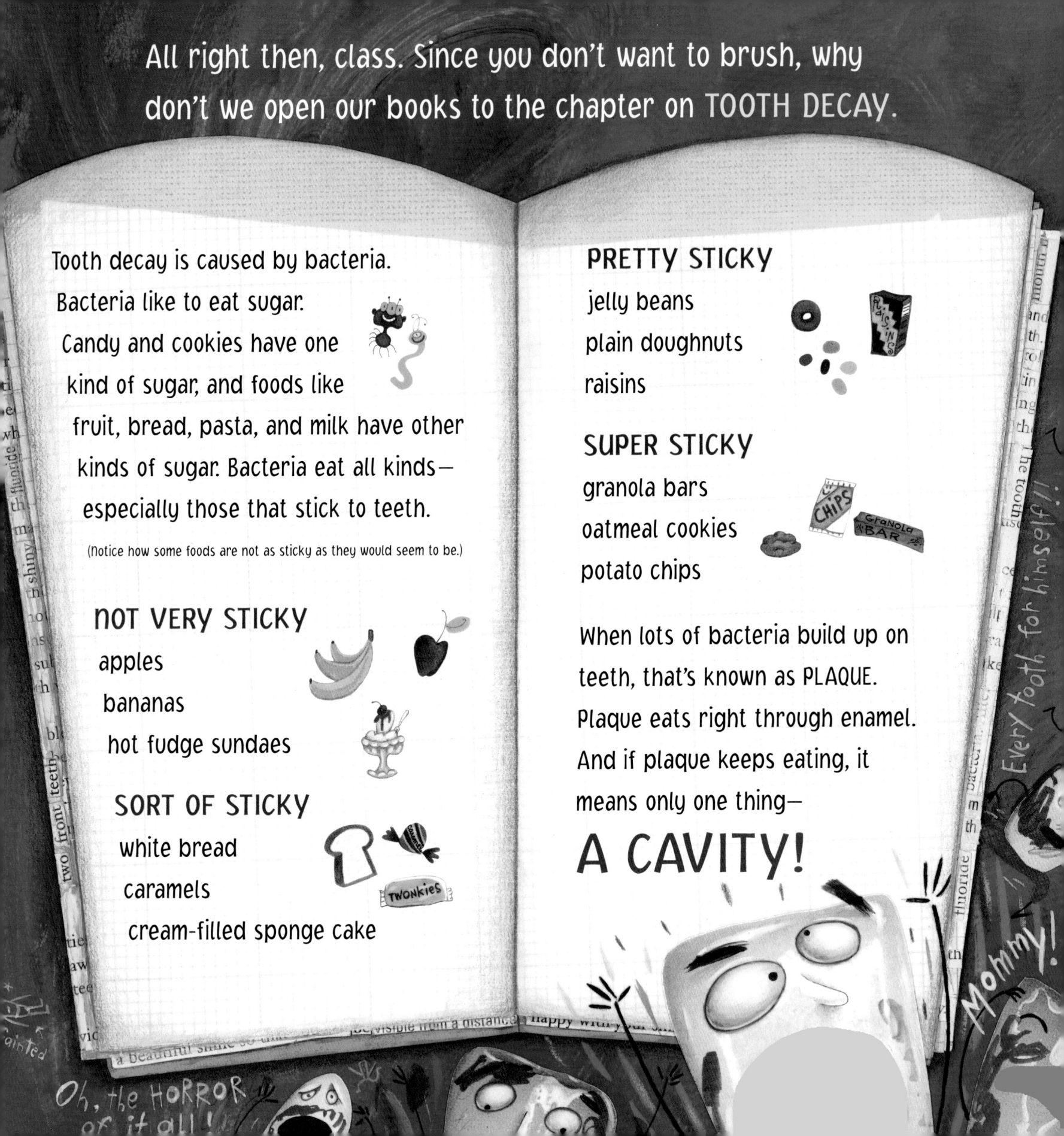

Now that's more like it, teeth.

Go get that bacteria!

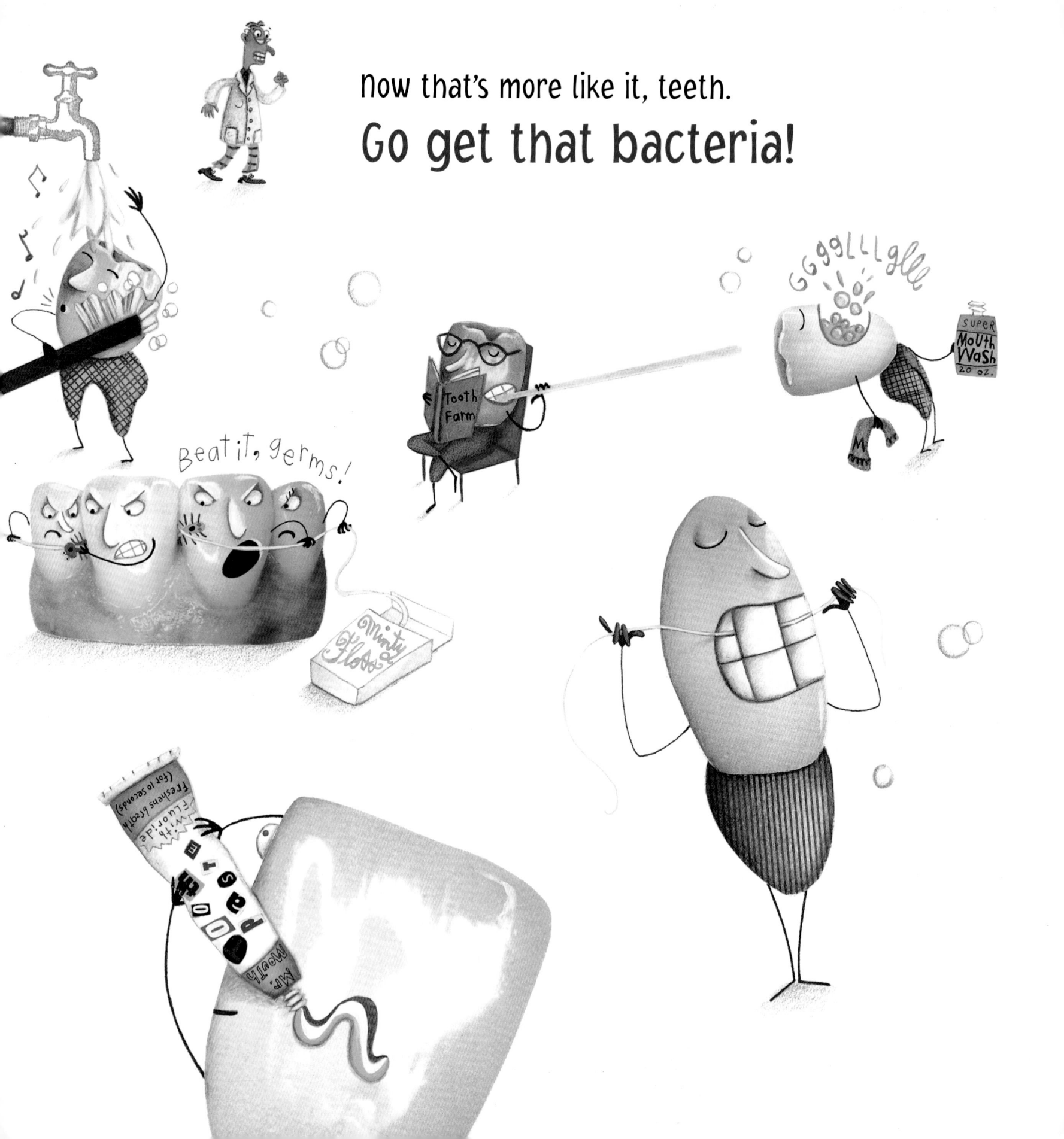

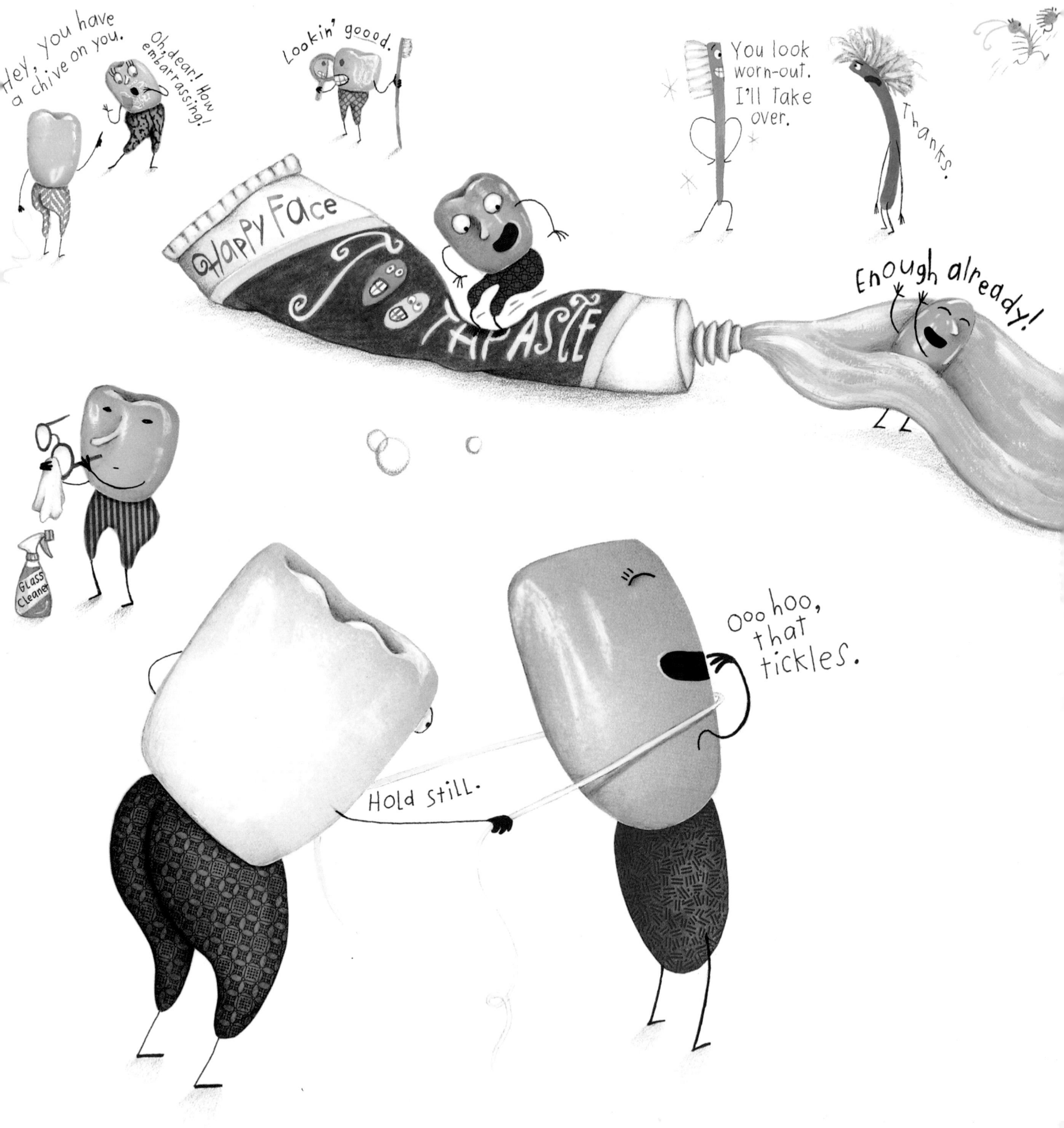
Hey, you have a chive on you.
Oh, dear! How embarrassing!
Lookin' goood.
You look worn-out. I'll take over.
Thanks.
Happy Face
Toothpaste
Enough already!
Glass Cleaner
Ooo hoo, that tickles.
Hold still.

OUR SELF-PORTRAITS
Dr. Flossman, my cousin got a cavity once, and he cried and cried like a big baby.
Well, Bubba Molar, a cavity can be painful. But a dentist can fix a cavity by drilling a hole into the damaged area of the tooth, clearing away the bacteria, and putting in a hard filling. Then it won't hurt anymore. And it's perfectly normal for a tooth to be frightened the first time it gets a cavity. Here are some common reactions:
I have bad breath.
Daddid he sssay ddddrill?
Umm, No— he said...uh... GRILL. Yeah, we're going to have a Cookout.

9 Common Reactions to Cavities*

SHOCK

PANIC

DEPRESSION

SELF-PITY

FEAR

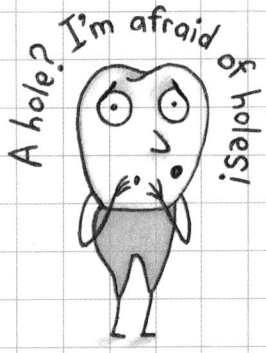

ANGER

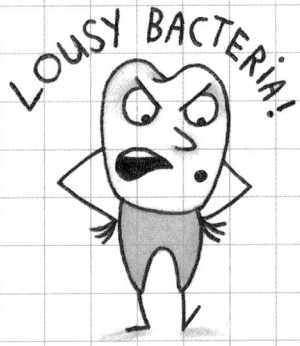

BLAME

DENIAL

ACCEPTANCE

*From the best-selling book *So You've Got Yourself a Cavity*, by Dr. Lou Stooth.

When a cavity is too small to see, a dentist will take an X RAY. An X ray can show the inside of a tooth. It makes cavities easy to see.

Don't you worry, teeth—brushing with fluoride toothpaste and flossing keeps away most plaque. But you should visit the dentist once or twice a year for a checkup to make sure you're healthy and clean.

An important reminder about dentists:

A **GOOD** dentist cleans and polishes teeth, and gives them a new toothbrush.

A **BAD** dentist skips work to play golf and sends his brother, the construction worker, to take his place.

I still love that one!

Ahhhaa haaha Ahhh

Haaa Haaaaa

Ahhh Haaaaahaha

Nice hair, Doc.

Charlie Premolar

Oh, please.

Lola Premolar

Not funny.

Martin Molar

Lame-o.

Rusty Molar

Ha Ha

Haha

TUESDAY

NDAY

TO

M

Sometimes, if teeth are CROOKED, a dentist will put braces on them to make them straight.

If a tooth gets BROKEN, a dentist can repair it with a tooth-colored plastic to make it look like new.

Class, I need to speak to the wisdom teeth for a minute in the hallway, but when I get back be ready to give your reports on teeth throughout history.

ELECT ROLAND MOLAR FOR STUDENT COUNCIL PRESIDENT
"The Right Tooth for the Job"
Noogie attack!
Ahh!
Break Glass in case of Emergency
Listen, I've really enjoyed having you wisdom teeth in class, but I'm going to pull you out and send you on to higher learning. You already know all this stuff and are probably bored out of your minds. You were the last four teeth in the mouth, but by far the wisest.
Go forth! Do great things!
To chew is to be.
If a tooth is traveling north at 50 mph...
I chew. Therefore, I am.

I'm back, class. So let's hear those reports.

Ancient Egyptians believed that a mixture of onion, spices, and incense would cure a toothache.

In the ninth century, Mayans filed their teeth into different shapes and decorated them with jewels.

In 1570, Queen Elizabeth received a gift of six gold toothpicks to clean her teeth.

In the early 1600s, Japanese women blackened their teeth to show loyalty to their husbands.

In the Middle Ages, Apollonia became the patron saint of dentistry. She said if someone with a toothache mentioned her name, the pain would go away.

In the 1500s, people could get their hair cut, wounds treated, and teeth pulled by their barber.

George Washington, the first president of the United States, had lots of dental problems. By 1796 he had lost all but one of his teeth. He had dentures made of elephant ivory, hippopotamus tusks, and cow teeth (not wood, as you may have heard). The dentures had sharp hooks, screws, and springs that made it hard for him to smile.

Excellent job, teeth! I'm so proud of you.

Well, rinse, gargle, and spit in a cup!
We're done for the day, teeth, so
I'll see you back here tomorrow.
Now don't forget your homework.

And don't forget to brush!

DUSTBALL
Hey, wait up!
NG!
classroom
to use
I like learning about me.
I hope I didn't forget anything.
YES— like I tell you EVERY DAY, we have to come back tomorrow!
Thanks for carrying my books.
YEAH, WHATEVER!
YIPPEE!
outta my way!
NOTEBOOK

True or False

1. Army soldiers protect teeth from bacteria and germs. T or F
2. Healthy teeth should be holey and green. T or F
3. Baby teeth guide permanent teeth into position. T or F
4. Fruit, bread, pasta, and milk have sugar in them. T or F
5. Bacteria like to eat sugar. T or F
6. A dentist can fix a cavity by putting a bandage on it and giving it a kiss. T or F
7. Teeth should have a checkup once or twice a year by a mechanic. T or F
8. An X ray can show the inside of a tooth. T or F
9. George Washington had teeth made out of rocks and twigs. T or F
10. Marshmallow is the softest part of the tooth. T or F

True or False Answers:

1. F; 2. F; 3. T; 4. T; 5. T; 6. F; 7. F; 8. T; 9. F; 10. F

Multiple Choice

1. How many permanent teeth are in the mouth?

   a. 4 b. 32 c. 97

2. What holds teeth in place?

   a. a root b. a boot c. a parachute

3. Primary teeth are also known as

   a. grumpy teeth b. baby teeth c. smelly teeth

4. The incisors are

   a. food throwers b. food wasters c. food cutters

5. After meals teeth should be

   a. painted purple b. brushed and flossed c. pulled out and put back in

6. Tooth decay is caused by

   a. bacteria and germs b. slugs and worms c. bad perms

7. If plaque builds up on teeth it can cause

   a. a thunderstorm b. a fight c. a cavity

Multiple Choice Answers:

1. b; 2. a; 3. b; 4. c; 5. b; 6. a; 7. c

The NIGHT of the KILLER CAVITIES
POP CORN
Hi, Chip.
Hey- what's that thing you're holdin' there?
It's called a TOOTHBRU
You migh want to t it same ti
Sweet Tooth
CHOCOLATE
Baby Tuth
Doughnuts
Is it me... or are we drifting apart?
HELLO, HANDY.
You can't HANDL the tooth

Tidbits
CONTOOTHIUS
(A WISDOM TOOTH)
Oh, Wise One, will I be a great, famous quarterback?
No. NEXT!
All right, so we LOST 112 to Nothing. Next time we'll CLOBBER 'em!
Rotten-Teeth Ralphie
"Don't make him smile!"
20 min. wait FROM HERE.
CONTOOTHIUS
NOON-5
Oh, dear— a Cavity! Why tonight?!
Mouth Wash
Ingrid Incisor
FLORIDA
I think I'm in the wrong book.
Hi there, Fluoride-A!
See You Tomorrow
They're auditioning for a movie— A Few Good Teeth.
Very Convincing.
Festive Root canal tree
DON'T MAKE ME COME BACK THERE!
Tooth School Bus
PRIVATE
the
complement
face.
loss
teeth
losses
efficiency

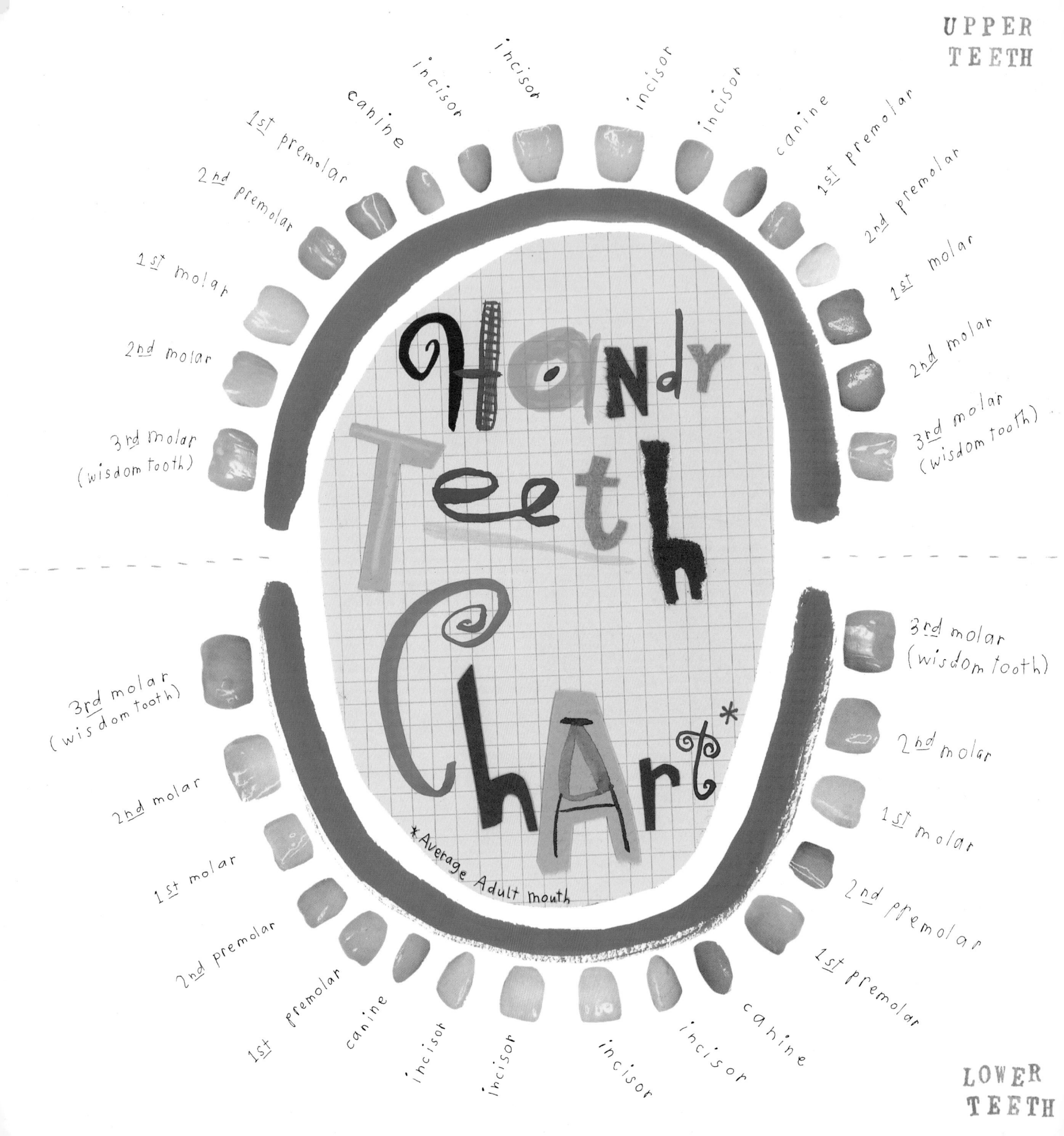
UPPER TEETH
incisor
incisor
incisor
incisor
incisor
canine
canine
1st premolar
1st premolar
2nd premolar
2nd premolar
1st molar
1st molar
2nd molar
2nd molar
3rd molar (wisdom tooth)
3rd molar (wisdom tooth)
Handy Teeth Chart*
*Average Adult mouth
3rd molar (wisdom tooth)
3rd molar (wisdom tooth)
2nd molar
2nd molar
1st molar
1st molar
2nd premolar
2nd premolar
1st premolar
1st premolar
canine
canine
incisor
incisor
incisor
incisor
LOWER TEETH

NOW THAT IS ONE HAPPY FLOWER!
LET A SMILE BE YOUR UMBRELLA

Laurie Keller

is the award-winning author and illustrator of *The Scrambled States of America*, *Arnie the Doughnut*, *Grandpa Gazillion's Number Yard*, and *Do Unto Otters: A Book About Manners*. She lives in Michigan.